THE TEDDY BEAR FAERIES

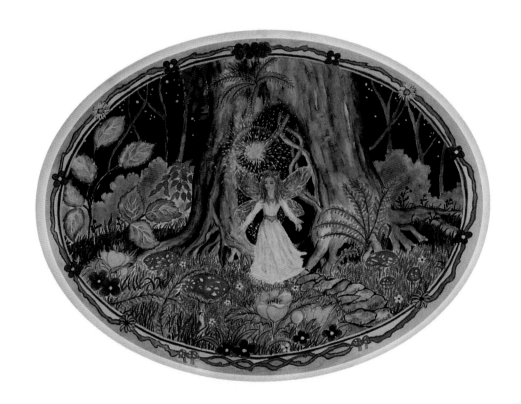

Written and illustrated by Ines E. de Castro

Book design by Elena / www.Websiteartwork.com

Book Publishers Network
P.O. Box 2256
Bothell • WA • 98041
Ph • 425-483-3040
www.bookpublishersnetwork.com

10 9 8 7 6 5 4 3 2 1

Printed in the United States of America

LCCN   2010918476
ISBN10 1-935359-72-x
ISBN13 978-1-935359-72-2

CPSIA facility code: BP 305980

To my son Christopher

It was a clear full-moon night. Christopher placed his teddy bear on the pillow next to him and settled into his bed.

*T*he teddy bear was brown and furry with a gleam in his eyes. What fun Christopher and the teddy had had during the day playing on the wooden floor of their room.

*C*hristopher woke up suddenly during the night. He thought he heard a noise in his room. He got up and saw that his teddy was gone. He looked out the window and saw a strange light in the wood behind the garden.

Christopher put on his robe and his slippers and left his house. He walked through the garden and followed the path that led into the wood.

He watched spellbound. Under the oak tree was a ring of toadstools. Upon each toadstool sat a lovely, silvery winged faery, beaming in a whirl of faerydust.

*H*is teddy bear and a whole column of other teddies, cream, tan, and grey were prancing about. They were marching around and around and in and out of the toadstool ring in rhythm.

The faeries stepped down from the toadstools. They held hands and formed a circle and danced and danced.

Christopher froze in amazement. Two grey rabbits and a deer came up to the circle and watched the dancing faeries.

*T*he next thing Christopher knew was that he was lying in bed. The sun was streaming in through the window, and the robins were chirping. What a pleasant dream he had had.

Christopher noticed his teddy bear was still gone. He was sure he had placed the teddy on the pillow next to him the night before. He looked on the floor, under the bed, in his closet and frantically rummaged through his toybox. The teddy bear was really gone.

He ran out of the house into the wood. There he found his teddy. The bear was sitting under the oak tree with that special gleam in his eye.

Ines de Castro was born in England where she grew up with faerie lore. She now lives in the Pacific Northwest with her son Christopher where she teaches Spanish German and French to students of all ages. She loves painting images from nature and from her imagination as well as themes from her worldwide travels to Europe, Asia, and Latin America. The Teddy Bear Faeries is her first published children's book. Her second book is about the travels of the unicorn Metzel.